**Give your child a head start with
PICTURE READERS**

Dear Parent,

Now children as young as preschool age can have the fun and satisfaction of reading a book all on their own.

In every Picture Reader, there are simple words, rebus pictures, and 24 flash cards to cut out and keep. (There is a flash card for every rebus picture plus extra cards for reading practice.) After children listen to each story a couple of times, they will be ready to try it all by themselves.

Collect all the titles in our Picture Reader series. Once children have mastered these books, they can move on to Levels 1, 2, and 3 in our All Aboard Reading series.

For Melissa, who likes witches
and cats—M.H.

Copyright © 1997 by Margaret A. Hartelius. All rights reserved. Published by Grosset & Dunlap,
Inc., a member of The Putnam & Grosset Group, New York. ALL ABOARD READING is a
trademark of The Putnam & Grosset Group. GROSSET & DUNLAP is a trademark of Grosset
& Dunlap, Inc. Published simultaneously in Canada. Printed in the U.S.A. Library of Congress
Catalog Card Number: 96-79104

ISBN 0-448-41614-X   B C D E F G H I J

A PICTURE READER

WHERE IS MY BROOM?

By **Margaret A. Hartelius**

Grosset & Dunlap • New York

It is time to get up!

Lizzy the

puts on her .

She puts on her .

She puts on her .

"Now I need my ,"

says Lizzy the .

"But where is my ?"

Lizzy the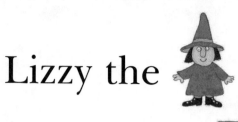

looks in her  .

She looks

behind her  .

She looks

under her  .

No !

"My  must be

in the kitchen,"

says Lizzy the .

She looks behind the .

She looks in the .

She looks under the .

No !

Maybe the 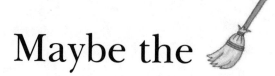 is in the living room.

Lizzy the looks behind a .

She looks under the .

She pulls up the .

No !

"I will ask the  ,"

says Lizzy the .

"Maybe he knows

where my is."

She goes out

to find the .

Lizzy the  looks

behind the .

She looks in the .

She looks up in the 🌳.

No 🐱!

No 🧹!

She climbs the

to the very top.

She sees a

of  .

But no  !

No  !

Something flies by!

"What is that?"

says Lizzy the  .

"Is it a  ?

Is it a  ?

Is it a  ?"

"No! It is that

on my !

Come down here!

Come now!"

shouts Lizzy the .

Swoosh!

Down comes that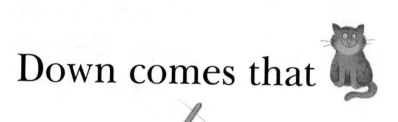

on the !

He scoops up Lizzy

the from the !

She flies up in the air.

She lands on the

behind the .

And they fly away

together!

dress	witch
hat	shoes
closet	broom

bed	dresser
cupboard	stove
chair	table

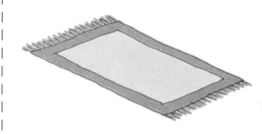

rug	couch
fence	cat
tree	bushes

birds	nest
plane	bird
leaf	rocket